H·N·I·C

H·N·I·C

BY ALBERT "PRODIGY" JOHNSON
WITH STEVEN SAVILE

Infamous

Published by Akashic Books
©2013 Albert "Prodigy" Johnson

Hardcover ISBN-13: 978-1-61775-236-0
Paperback ISBN-13: 978-1-61775-232-2
Library of Congress Control Number: 2013938811

First printing

Infamous Books
c/o Akashic Books
PO Box 1456
New York, NY 10009
info@akashicbooks.com
www.akashicbooks.com

ONE

BLACK SAID THAT IT WAS GOING TO BE EASY.
Black didn't know shit. He just acted like he did, and
no one questioned him.

The plan was simple: "We'll just go in there, and
when the shit gets real, we'll wave our guns around. Put
a couple of shots into the ceiling. Shout. I mean fuckin'
shout. Make a whole fuck of a lot of noise. We want to
scare the tellers and keep them scared. Scared people do
what you tell them. They don't think for themselves. And
we'll just tell them to put the money in the bags while the
piss runs down their legs."

Pappy was cool with that. Scaring was fine. He wasn't
cool with the whole gun thing: you pulled a piece if you
intended to use it, you didn't need the whole swagger
bullshit. Shooting the ceiling wasn't a mile away from
putting a cap in the girl behind the counter when she
was too frightened to fill the bag fast enough for your
liking. Things escalated. And Black was one unpredict-
able motherfucker. He was in it because of the thrill. He
loved the fucking rush. Best fucking high ever, he'd said

more than once. The money was just sugar. Sweet, sweet sugar, sure, but sugar just the same. Heat it up and it gets sticky and sickly and it stops being sugar. They were like that, Pappy and Black.

Pappy was all about the money. It wasn't about control or respect or fear, or any of those other things that fired Black's soul. It was all about the money.

And when the risk outweighed the reward it wasn't a risk worth taking. There was no glory in going out in a hail of bullets. Live fast, die young, and leave a beautiful corpse behind was nowhere near as appealing as not dying young and instead leaving an old and haggard one behind. Pappy wanted to *live*. Really live. Suck the marrow out of the bones of life. What was the good in being beautiful if you weren't around to fuck and sing and laugh and punch and, *fuck*, just all of that shit? A beautiful corpse would rot soon enough. So, no, it was about staying alive so long that he'd become the old nigga on the tenement stoop, smoking his liquorice-paper cigarette and blowing smoke rings while the kids fucked about, being kids.

And that meant using his head.

Loyalty was one thing, but it only went so far.

Getting yourself perforated just because you like a guy, or because you grew up on the same streets and fucked the same girls, sometimes alone, sometimes together, didn't make it smart.

"If I'm gonna do this, it's gonna be done right. No fucking around. It's gonna be big enough to cash out, man."

"Last job," Black swore, cursing it.

But Pappy meant it; this was the end of the road, the last job. From tomorrow his life was all about making a fresh start. He was getting out before hanging around with Black meant he wound up in the ground. He had a plan. It wasn't fully formed. He couldn't risk thinking about it too much. Daydreaming. He needed to be on his game. Right now all he knew for sure was come the morning he'd light out for Detroit. Clean start, different city. No one knew him out there. Maybe he'd even get himself into some computer school or something, make a real life for himself.

Black wouldn't give up this kind of life.

It was in his blood. Like poison.

Even if he decided to start again somewhere else, it wouldn't be long before he fell into the same patterns of behavior. That was just who he was.

"Down! On the *fuckin'* floor!" Black yelled as he pushed through the glass double doors into the bank.

He fired one shot after another into the ceiling, sending a shower of plaster drifting down like snow.

Hysterical shouts and cries filled the silence after the

shots. Someone sobbed uncontrollably. Black ignored them all.

Pappy dumped a bag in front of one of the tellers. He looked along the counter to see another bag go down. The ski masks made them all look the same. He almost laughed at the thought. It wouldn't be the first time a pretty white girl had been confused by color, after all.

Black stood in the middle of the floor, acting the big man, ready to explode: "I said stop your fuckin' noise, bitch!" Pappy glanced toward him. Black held his gun—a huge Desert Eagle—an inch from the face of an old woman. She was barely keeping it together and the gun wasn't helping.

"Hurry," Pappy told the teller, willing her to read his mind. If they didn't get out of here soon, things would go bad real fast.

He'd seen Black pumped up like this before.

There was no point trying to reason with him.

The best they could do was get out of there.

But fast was never going to be fast enough.

Someone was always going to try and be a fucking hero.

It was written in the stars.

In blood.

In that endless second between heartbeats it all went wrong.

A security guard, hyped on adrenaline and stupid Hollywood movies, made a grab for Black. He caught him around the neck, from behind, and pulled the mask from his head in the struggle.

Black lashed out violently, swinging the Desert Eagle like a club. The barrel hit the guard square in the temple with a sickening crunch. Something broke in there. Pappy heard it from where he stood. There was nothing good about that sound. He watched the man collapse.

Black scrambled for his mask, trying to cover his face again, but they all knew it was too late for that. Cameras had caught him now. There were dozens of them inside the bank; one would have captured a perfect picture of his face.

Black stood over the guard. He hawked and spat, then pulled the trigger. Once. Twice. Three times. The dead man's body only twitched a single time.

The alarm broke the stunned silence. The atmosphere in the bank changed with those shots. The hysteria was as dead as the guard. Every last one of the customers and staff stared with disbelief at the Desert Eagle, at Black, at the dead man, and knew that but for the grace of whatever god, devil, or deity they chose to believe in, it could have been them down there. It had just become very fucking real.

Pappy breathed deeply. Someone needed to take control.

This wasn't supposed to happen.

The plan was in, grab the cash, and out again—no one gets hurt. No one winds up dead.

But there he was, blood spilling out across the marble floor.

Pappy felt sick.

Banks were insured; they could afford to lose the cash. That guy down there was someone's son, someone's husband, someone's father. Or had been. Now he was just dead.

Pappy choked back the bile.

There was a split second where nobody moved. And then they started running for the door, all thoughts of the money abandoned. Now it was all about getting the fuck out of Dodge before the cops came in with guns blazing. Black was the first to run out. So much for that fucking loyalty shit. Pappy was last out, behind Ant.

Outside, Von had the engine running. As they all piled into the car, Black screamed at him to drive.

Tires screeched and he pulled into the fast-flowing traffic to the chorus of horns blaring as the car behind was forced to break hard to avoid a collision, only for an Econoline to ram him from behind. It was a piece of good luck, so maybe one of Black's demons was watching over them after all. The wreck would delay pursuit, and they only needed to cover a dozen blocks to abandon the stolen vehicle and switch it for the clean car that was parked and ready for them.

For Black that counted as forward thinking. It was, as he put it, a motherfucking plan. Black had a way with words. The reality of it was they could have been taken down before even leaving the bank. On another day they could have all been dead by now.

"So how much cash did we get?" Von asked as he pulled the second car carefully into traffic. Now it was all about not standing out. They could hear the sirens, so it wouldn't be long before the cops found the getaway car. They welcomed it; they'd be long gone by then.

Black said nothing.

Pappy could see the rage seething inside him, barely kept in check. It could have been down to the fact he'd left his face behind on the cameras, or the fact they'd walked out of the door as broke as they walked in. Pappy doubted very much that it was down to the fact Black had left someone dead on the cold stone floor.

"Come on, guys, how much? Enough for a trip to the sun? I'm ready for some of that sea, sand, sex, and shit, you know?"

"Will you shut the fuck up?" Black snapped.

"Nothing," said Pappy. "Not a fucking dime."

"Shut your fuckin' mouth, Pap, I need to think."

"Things didn't go down the way we planned," Ant said, as though that explained everything.

"What?"

"Just leave it, Von. It didn't work out. No sand, no sea, but give it a few minutes and you'll feel like you've been well and truly fucked, so it's all good."

Pappy knew one thing for sure: he wasn't waiting for tomorrow to head for Detroit. He was going tonight, cash or not. If he had to work nights in some shithole diner to see himself through college, then so be it. He wasn't proud. And washing pots wouldn't get him banged up for life. There was no fucking glamour in this life. Black was a dumb cunt. It was as simple and ugly as that. He'd seen enough to know the way things were going. He wanted out. That was the first smart decision he'd made since Sumner Houses. They weren't a fucking crew anymore. So they had managed to get out, it didn't matter; it wouldn't take *CSI* geniuses to determine who'd pulled the trigger, and Pappy wasn't about to spend the rest of his life looking over his shoulder. If the cops didn't get him, it was only a matter of time before Black did. That was Black's idea of covering his tracks.

Von pulled over at the lights.

"I'm out of here," Pappy said, climbing out of the car.

Black stared at him. He didn't say *Get back in*, he didn't say *See you around*. He just nodded.

"Last job," Pappy said, slamming the door.

"No looking back, Pap," Black responded, making a pistol with his fist and pulling the imaginary trigger.

TWO

PAPPY WAS STILL PACKING WHEN SOMEONE HAMMERED ON THE DOOR. Three a.m.

He'd read somewhere that more people die at that time than any other.

He didn't need to open the door to know it was Black.

The only question was whether or not he was on his own, or if he'd brought his little Desert Eagle friend along to say farewell.

There was no point in delaying it. He opened the door.

Black smiled at him. "Leaving so soon?" he said as he walked inside. He didn't wait to be invited in. He wasn't a fucking vampire—Pappy doubted a stake to the heart would have the slightest effect on him. You had to have a heart for that to work. Fuck, Pappy was surprised he'd bothered knocking in the first place. A bullet to the lock was as good as a key.

"You knew the score," Pappy said.

He could feel his heartbeat kick on.

They had been friends for years, but that didn't mean he was immune to Black's anger, only that he'd known him long enough to know to be afraid of him. "That was my last job. It's not fun anymore, we're into some fucked-up shit now."

"Fucked-up shit indeed, Pap, but that don't change things. You need a stash for that new life of yours. New living don't come cheap. Fuck, man, we both need the cash."

Pappy shrugged. "Not worth getting upset about."

"Ain't it? Tell me again why we were in that place. Oh, right, it was to give you the bucks to light out. We put our fuckin' stones out there for you, Pap. You can't just run out on us. Not now. You owe us. We need you with us, brother."

"I've had enough. Gotta move on, make a fresh start."

"You sound like a shit country-and-fuckin'-western song, Pap. Come back to mine for the night. Tonya'll cook up something good. We'll chill, shoot the shit like the old days. Make plans. Think big. The rest of the crew will be there. I'll get a few girls over. Make it a fuckin' party. Pretend like we're celebrating. See you off in style. My gift to you, bro. A proper goodbye. It's all sorted."

Pappy didn't want to go.

Really didn't want to.

He knew how it would go down.

But it wasn't a life that was easy to walk out on. They had history. They might not be blood, but they were more than just family.

He nodded.

One more night couldn't make any real difference. He'd be gone by first light. He'd still have time to say goodbyes.

"I'll be along later," he said.

"Nah, man, we go together. The car's outside, the motor's purring, and we have a driver who's getting to like sitting behind the wheel just a little too much and a couple of bitches in the back who can't sit still, if you dig. You and me, brother man. One last fuckin' time. You and me."

THREE

T HE CREW LIVED IN A HOUSE THAT HAD LAIN EMPTY FOR TOO LONG.
Finders keepers—and all that shit.
They'd just taken up residence and no one had tried
to move them out.

The whisper was the old guy who'd lived there had
died and his son was doing a seven stretch, so no one
would be coming home soon.

Black said he'd been given the okay to crash there,
but Black was full of shit. Still, no one came looking to
collect on any bills, and the neighbors steered as clear as
they would have if it were a crack house.

Pappy had never lived there. It had been important
to him from day one to be independent. His crib might
have been nothing more than a one-room bed-sit above
a takeaway, but it was *his* one room. It gave him a sense
of who he wanted to be.

Most of the floor space was taken up with books,
pieces of discarded computer equipment recovered from

dumpsters, along with a few more expensive kits boosted from electronics stores. While the others had gone for plasma TVs and stereo systems, he'd always had an eye for top-of-the-line computers.

He was self-taught, but that shit just made sense to him. It was a gift, but he knew that there was a lot more he could learn with the right sort of teacher. That was why he wanted to get himself out of this place. Funny thing was, there was more money to made by being legit than there was from a life of petty crime, and with that money there was a different kind of life, a different kind of respect.

People made a lot of noise about respect. Most of them didn't know what the word meant.

Pappy did. He wanted people to look up to him because they thought he was a golden fucking god when it came to what he did, not like they looked up to Black because they were afraid to look down while he pissed on their feet. It was a different kind of power.

It was the same with the girls, but in a different way.

Some of them were attracted to Black and the crew who surrounded him because they sensed his power. Some of them were drawn in by danger and the drugs— they went hand in hand. Some came for the cash, literally. So as it was stuffed into their thongs they'd moan and writhe and press up against the hand that fed, faking just how fucking hot the whole lie was. It was a house of lips, lies, and hips, and without Black it would all come tumbling down. He was the glue that stuck it all together.

Pappy walked through the front door, one pretty-looking bitch hanging off his arm. She was only there because Black had put her there. Pappy hadn't seen her before, and really wasn't in the mood to find out who she was. She clung to him like a clam. Black had no doubt promised her a snatch full of cash if she was nice to him. Nice. Right.

Tonya was different; she was with Black because she wanted to be, not because of what she got out of it in return. At least that was how it looked to Pappy.

She'd hung around with the crew for a couple of years. All too often she was stoned and barely able to walk on her impossibly high heels. Maybe that was how she survived. Pappy might have had a dream, but there was no guarantee someone like Tonya had one.

Or hell, maybe she had one once upon a time, but gave up on it along the way. The hood wasn't exactly a place of fairy tales. Still, Pappy liked her, and if he'd been her fairy godfather he'd have wished her a better hand in life than the one she'd been dealt.

She hadn't always been like this; everyone had a time before, a time when they still thought that anything was possible. Maybe that was why she treated him and Black differently than the rest of the crew. They went back. They remembered a time when she had still been all pretty and virginal and sang gospel in the church choir.

That was before her mother had died and she'd been passed from one relative who didn't really want her to another, until she found herself with an uncle who thought that putting a roof over her head allowed him some God-given right to stick it in her like any God-fearing fucker would. So, yeah, maybe she'd had a dream before. It wasn't impossible, just life and a fat bastard had fucked it out of her.

Black had a dream too. Or so he said: fast cars, speedboats, a fucking *Miami Vice* soundtrack playing in his head as a beautiful bitch sucked on his cock. That was his version of heaven.

Looking at Tonya just made Pappy all the more determined to hang onto his dreams.

Once they were gone, they'd be impossible to find again.

He looked at his watch. Three thirty.

The first bus out to Detroit left at seven. He was going to be on it.

"I thought you were splitting, Pappy," Tonya said. She slurred her words a little. Her eyes were glazed. It was a permanent state of affairs.

"Soon enough," Pappy replied.

"He don't want you to leave, you know," she said, like it was some great secret. "Fool needs you around more than he can say."

The thing was, after today it didn't matter what Black wanted anymore. It was all about what Pappy needed from now on.

It had to be.

Someone passed him a bottle of bourbon.

He sank down onto a leather sofa. The stitching sighed—it had seen its best days end with Reagan.

Despite everything, he felt comfortable here. Sometimes home didn't have to be home. Sometimes it just had to be a good, safe place. And this was as good a place as any to spend his last night in town.

And no matter what else, Black knew how to party.

Someone turned the music up. Bass drove the rhythm—hard, pounding, incredibly sexual. This was the music of life. This was the hammer of life. Raw. Primal. The words bled into each other and he could imagine the guy, oil-slick skin, tats like tribal markings, girls coiled like snakes around his well-defined physique.

Pappy lost himself in it for a moment, grateful to forget the failure of the day. The music grew louder. He closed his eyes, felt his body shake with it. Sometimes he couldn't express himself—he wasn't good with words, he couldn't say what he wanted to, not in the same way he could put something into a computer and make the thing dance to whatever tune was in his head. He wasn't a words guy. But sometimes he could imagine himself up there, the guy behind the mic rapping out from his soul, reaching people. Making them understand. And then there were days like today, when getting wasted seemed like the best fucking idea in the world and a viable way out that didn't involve applying to some IT department in some school where his gang tats wouldn't serve as a reference.

He felt a hand on his thigh, then it moved on to his cock, stroking gently, insistently, and breath on his ear, warm, hungry.

She bit at his ear, and pressed down harder, grinding up against him.

"You're such a cliché," he said, without opening his eyes.

"And you fucking love it," she whispered.

It was hard to argue with that.

He heard shouting somewhere, but didn't feel like going to investigate. Let the fuckers have at it. If it kicked off then he'd know soon enough, and that would be too soon, given what her hand was doing. He didn't even know her name.

Then there was a scream.

Then silence.

Whoever played deejay just turned the volume up, drowning out the sobs. He opened his eyes eventually with a damp patch in his lap that wasn't from the bourbon.

The girl was gone.

There was no sign of Tonya or Black.

He saw Von and Ant arguing in the corner.

The crew.

No matter how much he tried to convince himself otherwise, he was going to miss the niggas he grew up with.

Gee had crashed out in an armchair with a naked Latina curled up in his lap. She had spectacular tits and very little else going for her.

Pappy pushed himself up out of the sofa. The stale air was playing havoc with his head. Fuck knows what was floating in it. He needed some fresh air.

He went over to the window and cracked it open. Fresh air—or as fresh as the shithole that was the city allowed—filled his lungs. He counted to ten, exhaling on each number.

When he turned around he saw Tonya standing behind him. She had swelling around one eye and a smear of blood—already dried—staining her lower lip and chin like kids' makeup. There was nothing cute about the image.

"Fuck, Ton," he said, reaching out to touch her cheek, "you okay?"

She tried to force a smile. Even he could see it hurt. She had tears in her eyes. He started to instinctively hold her in his arms, but then he saw Black in the doorway, face like thunder.

"You and me, we need to talk, Pap," Black said. He inclined his head toward the door, beckoning Pappy to follow him out of the room.

Black had that bug-fuck crazy look in his eye. It was a look that Pappy knew well. Now wasn't the best time to stand up to him. Pappy took another glance at Tonya, but she didn't peer back at him.

The bedroom stank of stale smoke and hot sweaty sex. There was no smell in the world like it. It filled up every inch of the place. Alive. It smelled alive. Pappy felt Black's eyes boring deep into him. Pappy didn't move. He waited for Black to say something. Black shook his head. Pappy felt the sweat trickle down his back. His empty stomach shrunk down to a fraction of its size.

"Tonya says I should just let you fuck off and follow your dreams," he said, finally, as though it was the craziest shit he'd ever heard.

"We've had this conversation. I've always said I was going. This place, the whole fucking thing, it's not me, man. Not anymore."

"I know it's what you *said*, Pap. But saying and do-ing, they're two different things, nigga. You're my boy. We're like this"—he crossed his fingers and put them over his heart—"and I need you here, man, you gotta keep me straight. I'll go fuckin' under without you, Pap."

"I'm sorry, man, I'm done."

"No." Black shook his head. "You're done when I say you're done. One last job. That fuckin' shit today wasn't a job, it was a fuckin' piece of shit. You owe me a job. A proper fuckin' score. I need it, man."

"I'm not listening to this shit, Black. Get out of my fucking face, I'm out. Done. Over."

Black stared him in the eye. "You owe me, bro. One last job. I can't do it without you."

"I'm not listening."

"Of course you fuckin' are. You haven't pushed me out of the way, have you? No you fuckin' haven't, so cut the bullshit, nigga. We get this one right and I'm gone for good. We both get the life we want. Think about it, Pap. One job. A few fuckin' hours of your life. You owe me that. We both know I'm fucked. That stupid fuckin' guard ruined my fuckin' life. I'm fucked. I mean, prop-er fucked. Any second now the fuckin' law will come knocking on the door. They've seen my face on the CCTV. I can't stay here. This ain't no fuckin' fortress of solitude, Pap, it's a fuckin' squat. And I'm no fuckin'

Superman, you dig? It won't take them long to find out who I am."

Pappy didn't argue.

"Some fancy computer will go *ping* and my name will pop out and they will be looking for me. I need this job now so I can get out of town."

"What part of *I'm done* don't you understand?"

"The part where you think you're saying no to me, bro. Plain and simple, you ain't saying no. I can't do this without you, and like I said, you owe me. I've been pulling your sorry ass out of the shit since Sumner Houses."

"The only thing you've been pulling is your own cock, bitch."

Black laughed. Hard. "Man, Pap, I'm gonna fuckin' miss you when you're dead."

Pappy shrugged. "Why the fuck should I, man?"

"Because it's me, Pap." Black held out his hand. "Help me, Obi-Fuckin'-Pappy Kenobi, you're my only hope."

"Fuck you," Pappy laughed. "Obi-Fucking-Pappy Kenobi? Who's that make you? Princess Black?" He shook his head.

"Whatever it takes to get the job done."

"No guns," Pappy said, suddenly serious.

"Man, you don't even need to *be* there. I just need you to do the shit you do with your computers to fuck with an alarm system, so I can get in and get out quiet as a fuckin' church mouse, bro."

"I could do that from anywhere."

"You could, but I need you close."

"You don't trust me?"

"Jeez, dude, that's not what I'm saying. I need my people close. I like to be able to see what the fuck's occurring as it's fuckin' occurring, simple as that."

Black obviously wasn't going to make it easy for him to walk away.

"How soon?"

"Couple of days."

"Then we cut the cord, man. Separate ways."

Black nodded. "A week max. I've been planning this for ages, I can't do it without you. If I could, I would, I swear. And like I said, I'd really fuckin' miss you if you were dead, man. Know what I mean?"

Pappy was already starting to think in terms of what real difference a couple of days would make, and how useful the extra cash would be, and he hated himself for it. Every time it seemed like he was seriously getting his shit together and hauling out, Black just reeled him back in with some desperate fucking promise.

"What's a few more days?"

Black put a hand on Pappy's neck and pulled him close. Pappy could smell sour whiskey and what he assumed was Tonya's pussy juice on Black's breath. He wanted to pull away. He had never felt quite so uncomfortable with the man, or with knowing just what Tonya's honey smelled like. Black was like the sun . . . no . . . he was a fucking black hole. He just pulled you in and pulled you in until he consumed you, just like he'd consumed Ton.

"Just don't try to fucking kiss me, nigga," Pappy said.

Black barked out a laugh. "I knew I could count on you, Pap. Respect," he said, his fingers digging in too deep for comfort before releasing him.

Pappy caught himself before he rubbed the back of his neck. He didn't want to show any sign of weakness. And pain was weakness.

FOUR

THE CREW SAT IN THE CAR.

It was about as intimate as a rectal probe.

They watched the back roller doors of the jewelry depot as the armored security van pulled up. The doors were covered in layers of inventive graffiti.

They were away from the busy streetfront where those lovers pressed their faces up against the glass and pointed out the rings they wanted to tie the rest of their lives together with.

One of the guards—in a blue helmet that made him look like a crash-test dummy—climbed down out of the front and walked around to the back. He glanced around, then banged on the doors.

"He's looking, but the dumb fuck's not seeing anything," Black said. He was grinning fiercely.

"We should just do the van when they come for their next delivery," Pappy said.

Black shook his head. "Nah, man, watch and learn."

The back of the van opened and a second guard

stepped out. He was overweight and had a case chained to his wrist.

It was starting to look a fuck of a lot easier than Black had made it out to be: take down the guard, cut the chain with a pair of bolt cutters, disappear into the city with a case of precious stones. They didn't need Pap for it. He was starting to feel like he'd been played.

"So how much is in the case?" Gee asked from the other side.

"Who knows?" said Black. "This place gets a delivery every few days, more or less the same time of day. Maybe if we took the van we'd strike lucky and get it the day it's bringing in a case of diamonds from Amsterdam. You know, like in the movies, uncut stones, untraceable. Worth a fuckin' fortune. But maybe we'd get a box of engagement rings, or worse, just the rings, no stones yet. This is a one-shot deal. We get inside, we get more than anybody could ever need."

"Easy, man," Ant said, like he had a fucking clue.

Companies who had stuff this valuable maintained a high level of security. They'd have electronic systems in place. Stuff that shut the whole place down tight as Sister Mary Theresa's puckered cunt. They'd have guards and those guards would have guns, not nightsticks. Guns they'd be more than happy to use, and call it justifiable homicide if a nigga went down. No, this was a whole different ball game.

"I don't like it," Pappy said.

"Good thing you're not going inside then, Pap. Leave it to the big boys."

"So what's the plan?" Ant asked, like Black had all the answers.

"We go in through the door at night. I'm thinking an acetylene torch."

"What about the alarms?"

"That, bro, that's where Pappy comes in. He works his fuckin' magic and it's all quiet. So, Pappy, you think you can do something about the alarms?" He pointed at the yellow box on the wall. The worn-out sticker in the middle of it declared that the property was protected by Amerisafe Security. The same Amerisafe Security whose van was currently parked at the back of the building.

"Maybe," Pappy said.

"I need better than maybe, nigga. I need yes."

"Okay, yes, but it might take time."

"We ain't got time. We're hitting the place tonight."

"Tonight? But we're not ready."

"Don't worry. I've got everything we need. You just need to take care of the alarm. If it goes off, the whole thing's fucked and we're fucked right along with it."

"I don't care, it still doesn't give me enough time."

There was a giggle from beside him. Von had sparked up.

Pappy wound the window down to let the fresh air in. Black took the hint.

"Put that fuckin' thing out, you fuckin' stupid bitch. See, that's why white people always calling blacks dumb niggas."

Without a word, Ant crushed the joint in his bare hand and threw it out the open window.

Pappy could still walk away.

But if he did, he knew who was going to take the full brute force of Black's temper: Tonya. He'd already seen the blood and bruises that suggesting he should get to live his dream had earned her.

So, no, he couldn't walk away.

"There'll still be guards," Pappy said. No one else seemed to be remotely interested in the practicalities of the job, they just listened to what Black had to say and followed his instructions like sheep. No, not sheep, they were his own private army, ready to kill or be killed. Hoo-rah!

"Of course, but we'll have enough to deal with them."

"You, Gee, Ant, and Von? Four of you?" Pappy said, not believing him for a minute. "It doesn't add up." And it didn't. If Black was going in with the three men in the backseat, it didn't take a rocket scientist to know it wasn't going to be enough, even if he didn't leave Von in the van ready to drive.

Black gave him a long hard look. It was the kind of look that could take down a line of riot cops. Despite all of his promises, Pappy expected Black to tell him he was going in with them.

"It's not a problem, bro. I've got a specialist driver coming in, and he's bringing in a couple a goons. They can deal with any guards if it gets lively. You just worry about the alarm. Let me worry about everything else. You said that you don't want to be on the inside and that's cool, man. Cool. We good?"

"Everything's good," Pappy said, but it wasn't. Far from it.

Alarm bells were already starting to ring. These ones weren't Amerisafe Security, they were pure Pappy, pure self-preservation.

Black had only ever used the crew, never outsiders. They'd known each other since Sumner Houses, meaning forever. They were guys who'd watch each other's backs even when they were fucked out of their heads; it was instinct. They were a pack. Like wolves. The fact he now wanted to bring in outsiders reeked. Why now? Why, when they were lining up their biggest score ever?

It was suicide.

"I don't care how many bodies go in, so long as there's enough in the pot to divvy up when we make the split," Ant said, helpfully. He hadn't changed in all of those years since Sumner Houses. He was like a big dopey kid, only rather than being cute he'd grown up dangerous. "I wanna get me one of those big Caddies, pimp that fucker out, jack up the suspension. Big sound system in the back. I want people to hear me coming and stop to fucking look, you know what I'm saying?"

Black turned in his seat and said very slowly and very seriously, "You ain't spending a fuckin' dime until I'm outta this place. You want to get yourself busted after that, be my fuckin' guest, shithead, but don't expect me to come running to save your skinny ass, 'coz I'll be long gone."

"Maybe I'll come with you then," Ant said. "Get me some good times. See how we roll, Ant and Black, Black and Ant. Good times."

"Good times," Black laughed, but Pappy didn't think that he was laughing at the thought of the good times at all. There was something dark about it. "I guess we've seen all we need to see. I've got some business to take care of."

FIVE

THE ONE-ROOM APARTMENT HAD BEEN HIS MOTHER'S.
There was less than a week left on the lease.
Alone, Pappy flexed his fingers and began to type.

Computers weren't like people; they were logical, they had patterns built into them, lines that if you followed went from A to B and did exactly what you expected them to do. It wasn't like in the movies where some genius could take over the world at the stroke of a key, but if you knew what you were doing you could cause a world of hurt for someone.

Right now it was basic stuff, fact-finding, just like they'd scouted the jewelry depot. It was the same principle. He wanted to understand exactly how the alarm system worked, what would trigger it, and how to circumvent it.

Of course, it wasn't going to be easy.

It wasn't like he could just dial up the security company and ask for the password he'd need for remote access to their system.

But he knew what he was doing.

He pinged their network, which was a bit like knocking on the front door, and in return received a screenful of raw data that basically asked who he was, while expecting a digital handshake back from his machine. Pappy smiled. Sometimes failure was the quickest way to success. He deliberately pushed a little too hard, and was rewarded by a warning screen: *Unauthorized Access Attempt Detected*.

Excellent, Pappy thought to himself.

It wasn't as though they could follow it back to him; he'd rerouted his IP through a dozen anonymous servers set up in different countries, all outside of the US and hostile to the US government. He simply piggybacked their network, kind of like digging an electronic tunnel into a subnetwork that ran all around the world. All anyone in Amerisafe Security would know was that someone somewhere was trying to log in to their system—and very clumsily. It was important he looked like an amateur. The less of a threat his intrusion seemed, the less likely they'd be to alert the authorities. No harm, no foul. After all, it wasn't like it was a serious attempt to commit a crime.

His ma, God rest her soul, had always said there were more ways than one to skin a cat, and a lifetime of skating by had taught him that sometimes it was best to just go with the flow and follow the lines of least resistance. That was never more appropriate than now.

Pappy knew that it would be easy enough to physically cut the alarms, but that would mean being on site, and any sort of physical assault on the system was bound to trigger a silent alarm straight back to the head office of the security company, giving them maybe five minutes to get in and out before the cops showed.

He wasn't about to do that. Fool me once, shame on you; fool me twice, and I've got to be the prize motherfucking idiot. Black. Guns. New crew. All added up to: no. This was strictly arm's-length. If it went to hell then he'd be a million fucking miles away.

He tapped out a few more keystrokes, sending another string of data to the network. He arched his back, stretching, as the page loaded. The thing about computer crime was not reinventing the wheel. If he wanted to get in somewhere, chances were someone else had already tried to do the same thing. All he needed to do was walk a mile in their shoes. So, instead of hammering on the system's door, he logged into a hacker BB, and phrased a very loose query about digital handshakes with the system he was working with, which picked up an answer from Pakistan in less than sixty seconds, directing him to a guy who'd exploited a weakness in the SSL certification Amerisafe utilized to protect their system, and a downloadable file link.

He left a thank-you message, and within a minute had downloaded and installed the exploit, and was soon looking at the feed from the CCTV cameras inside the unit, his big shit-eating grin reflecting back at him from the screen. He could see exactly what they could, live, as it happened. He was a ghost in their machine. He checked the space on his hard drive, which was nowhere near what he needed for what he had in mind, and plugged in a 3TB external drive. He tapped out another command line and triggered the recording, storing every minute of today's footage on his drive. Come tonight he'd replay it, and they could all sit and watch a little bit of history while Black and the crew got on with the job. It was a gamble, but the beauty of internal footage meant there was no change in the natural light. They'd never spot the fact that the feed was from the day shift.

So now all he needed to worry about was the alarm itself.

He was all set to turn his attention to that very problem when a gentle knock at the door completely derailed his train of thought.

It wasn't Black, clearly. Black would have just walked right in. Ant, Von, even Gee would probably have yelled his name through the letter box.

The knock came again. It was a little more urgent the second time.

He opened the door.

Tonya's bruises had turned dark blue and no amount of makeup could hide them completely. Her lips still looked sore. Pappy thought the slightest smile would crack the wound open again.

He stepped aside and let her in.

He didn't know what to say, so he kept it simple: "Drink?" He cleared boxes from one of the chairs so she could sit down.

It was painfully obvious he was ready to leave. Everything was packed up and stacked, ready to be sent on to his final destination, wherever that may be.

She moved uncertainly, favoring her right side. Pappy realized that the bruised face and cracked lip were not the worst of her injuries.

Tonya shook her head and then closed her eyes, obviously regretting the suddenness of the motion. He killed the screen, but left the connection live, then turned the chair he had been sitting on to face her.

"You okay?" he asked. It was a dumb question.

She looked at him as though to say: *What the fuck do you think?* "Just needed to get out. Clear my head, you know." She shrugged.

"Sure, I know what you mean."

"He's going to make me drive," she said. Just like that. No preamble. *He's going to make me drive.* Pappy thought: *Fuck. Fuck. Fucking fucker.* "He lied to you. He doesn't have anyone else coming in on this job. It's all lies. Don't do it, Pappy. When he comes knocking, don't answer the door. Just go. Now. Please. This is all wrong. He's changed. I don't know what's wrong with him, but he's not right, Pappy. I've got a bad feeling about this."

"I'm not going inside."

"He won't give you the choice."

Pappy ignored her. "You don't have to do this, Ton. Break away. It's your life, you control how you live it. Don't let the bastard fuck you up anymore than he already has." He reached out, cupping her bruised cheek with his palm.

She started to cry. All it took was that one simple tenderness. She pulled a crumpled tissue from the pocket of her jeans. "He'll make me do it. I've tried to say no to him before. He won't listen."

"Is that why he did this to you?"

She shook her head. "No. He did this because I told him to let you go."

"Why would you stand up for me?"

"Because you're my friend," she said. It was the simplest answer of them all, and it went all the way back through their lives to the first time they'd met. It was the one answer he couldn't argue with.

He didn't even have to think about it. "I've got some

money set aside. It's yours. Take it. Get the fuck out of here, Ton. Get away from him." And he meant it. He would have willingly given every cent he'd saved if it meant she'd be safe.

She shook her head. "Don't worry about me. He's promised me that once this job's over we'll be heading out of town."

"Is that what you want?"

She shrugged again. "What's that got to do with anything?"

"Ton, I'm serious. You don't have to do this. Promise me you won't go on the job with them."

"I don't have a choice."

"Yes you do." He stared at her and realized something. It wasn't just about offering her money; he'd put himself in the firing line if it meant she'd be safe. "I'll go," he said.

"You can't. I can't ask you to do that. No. Please. Don't make me be the reason . . . Get out of here, Pappy. Don't fuck your life up for me. I can't be the reason."

"Maybe you don't have a choice, Ton. Maybe none of us have a choice. Maybe this is just the way it's meant to be. Written in the stars and all that BS."

Life was about hard choices.

He'd just made one.

Maybe now she'd be able to make one too.

That was the best he could hope for—that he'd at least give her the chance to make her own choices.

Tonya tried to hold back the tears. In that moment he realized she was always going to be Black's girl, no matter how badly he fucked her up. It was an addiction.

Part of him wanted to tell her that everything would be all right, but it was only a small part of him.

The rest of him, the parts he did his thinking with, didn't want to lie to her.

SIX

A SINGLE FLOODLIGHT ILLUMINATED THE BACK OF THE BUILDING. They rolled to a stop, killing the van's engine. The dashboard clock said, *12:15*. The streets were deserted. This wasn't the kind of district that teemed with nightlife. It was businesses, offices, warehouses. Quiet places, all shut up for the night.

There would be patrol cars cruising the area, but if they didn't get a callout, they'd not be expecting trouble. It wasn't the kind of place an opportunistic thief would strike. No, round here, the law enforcement would rely on the efficiency of alarm systems and private security firms. Or at least that was what he was counting on.

"All good, Pappy?" Black asked, and not for the first time.

"All good," Pappy said. He'd already gone over his side of the plan, piping the day's recording through the monitors in place of a live feed. Black had nodded and made out like he had a fucking clue what Pappy was talking about.

Even from the inside, dealing with the silent alarm

had been a little more complicated. The solution, when it came to him, had been nothing short of brilliant in its simplicity. He didn't have the kit to go all *Ocean's Eleven* on it, and as much as he'd love to pretend he was Neo and could just plug in and ride the waves of the Matrix, all that shit was, well, shit.

Instead of trying to find a way to *stop* the system, which would probably have set off all sorts of alarm bells, he'd simply gone into the route directory and changed the destination the alarm was being sent to. He picked out a unique IP that was only a couple of digits different: a Chinese restaurant in Delaware. If he was right, and he was gambling on the fact that he was, the system diagnostics would show that an alarm had been triggered, and the message dispatched. They'd be long gone before anyone realized something was wrong.

"What happened to the other guys you were bringing in?" Pappy asked.

"Chickened out. Fucking fags."

"More for us," Gee said. Pappy wanted to smack the fool. But then, maybe they'd always known there would be no one else?

"We got nice new guns though," Von laughed. He was sitting at the wheel, but Black had already decided there'd be no one left behind. When they went in, they'd storm the place together. One unit. Brothers in arms.

And they were armed to the teeth—though Pappy had no intention of firing his, no matter what went down in there.

"Well, let's do this, shall we?" Black said. He pulled the ski mask down over his face and opened the door.

The others did the same.

But keeping their identities secret was going to be the least of their problems.

Pappy was far from convinced an acetylene torch would cut through the door, for a start. Surely it was going to be armor-plated, and several inches thick. The lock would secure it with at least five bolts firing deep into the masonry. He shook his head.

"You really sure you can get through this, Von?"

It was Black who answered: "Not going to have to. We've got a key."

"A key? There's no keyhole, dude," Pappy said, then felt a sudden surge of panic as headlights lit up the parking lot. A car swung around and pulled in next to the van.

Black's car.

Tonya was behind the wheel.

Black smiled and walked toward her.

His Desert Eagle hung loose in his hand.

He wrapped an arm around her as she stepped out of the car and pulled her close. He kissed her hard, pushing the barrel of the gun between her legs. Pappy felt a surge of jealousy, and beneath it an undercurrent of fear. This whole thing had nothing to do with affection or passion; this was Black clearly marking his territory. He might as well have pissed on her like a dog.

Black let her go after what felt like a lifetime, but kept an arm around her waist as he moved with her around the car.

He popped the trunk.

Tonya stepped away from him, cast a glance Pappy's way.

Black reached into the trunk and pulled out a man in a suit. The guy had trouble standing, because his hands and feet were bound. He had a gag stuffed in his mouth, one of those gimp balls.

Black waved Pappy over and handed him a knife. "Cut him free." The guy's suit pants stank of piss.

"This, boys"—Black barked a brutal laugh, keeping a tight grip on the man's neck—"is our key to the kingdom. We made a deal, Mr. Henderson and me. He's going to open the door for us, and in return I'm not gonna fuck his wife and kid before putting a bullet in their heads. We both think it's a good deal, don't we, Mr. H?"

"Jesus fucking Christ, nigga, this shit's fucked," Pappy said, peering down at the knife in his hands. He could end it all here and now, one quick brutal thrust into the side of his friend's neck and everyone else could walk away.

Tonya got back in the car and drove off.

Pappy didn't move.

He was starting to feel again like he'd been played.

It wasn't a nice feeling.

Black removed the gag. "Okay, Mr. H, why don't you be a good little boy and get this door open so we can all go home?"

Henderson shuffled like a zombie toward the door. Von seemed to be enjoying the sight of the guy trying to keep his shit together and failing.

He fumbled in his pocket for a keycard, then slid it into a slot and tapped a six-digit code into the keypad. Six digits? Date of birth. Probably the kid's. That was how people worked. "Please," Henderson said, "please, I've done everything you've asked. Don't hurt them."

There was an almost inaudible buzz as the electrical contacts were released and the door jumped half an inch, popping open.

"Let's not get ahead of ourselves," Black said, pushing Henderson inside with the Desert Eagle. "Now the alarm." The beeping was already beginning to escalate, demanding to be silenced. "And don't think about being clever. 'Coz that'd be particularly dumb, man. Dumb gets people fucked and dumb gets people killed. Don't go putting that code in backward or any shit or I'll drop you where you stand." Putting the code in backward would silence any physical alarm, but it would also trip a silent distress signal. "No way out of here but my way."

But was there any way out for the guy?

He'd seen Tonya, and probably Black. The fact he could ID them meant he wasn't walking away from the depot. If Pappy knew it, Henderson had probably worked it out for himself. He had nothing to gain by helping them, and more importantly, nothing to lose by fucking with them.

Pappy knew he should walk away. Right then. Just turn and walk.

He didn't.

"There are two guards inside," Black said. "Top floor. They'll be coming down any minute. Let's wait for them to join us. Give them a big warm welcome." He tapped the barrel of the Desert Eagle to his cheek, the warmth of the welcome implicit.

They heard the hollow clang of footsteps on the steel stairs.

A minute later a guard emerged from the door. There was a moment, a single second, filled purely with confused silence, then Black pressed his gun into Henderson's cheek.

"All right, you cunt, this is how it's gonna play out.

You're gonna do everything I say, no fuckin' questions, or every fucker here's gonna fill you with so much lead your jizz'll glow in the dark." The guard didn't move. Black didn't move. "Now, nice 'n' fuckin' slow, take your gun and put it on the ground, then kick it toward me. Okay?"

The guard did as he was told.

Von stepped forward and claimed the weapon, tucking it in the back of his jeans. The guard glanced up at a CCTV camera and told his partner to get his ass down there, now.

"That wasn't very fuckin' clever, you dumb cunt," Black said, shaking his head. "Good thing I don't need to keep you alive, ain't it? Now shut the fuck up."

SEVEN

PAPPY DIDN'T LIKE IT.

It was too easy.

The guards were compliant. The second man had come barreling down the stairs, seen Black and the Desert Eagle, and dropped his gun on the spot. The vein at his throat and temple pulsed and every ounce of color drained out of his body in a split second. The poor fuck looked like he was having a coronary. That didn't stop Black from pistol-whipping him around the side of the head. The guy hit the ground and didn't move.

"On your knees, you funny fucker," Black told the other one. "Execution time."

The man went down, lowering his head like he expected a bullet in the brain. Von came up behind him and pulled plastic ties around his wrists, securing his hands behind his back. He did the same to the guy sprawled out on his fat belly.

"No one's gotta die then—shame, I was itchin', you know . . . Hey, H, maybe it'll be you, eh? Wanna get that fuckin' safe open before I get impatient?"

Henderson didn't say anything.

He was on his knees, trying to open the small safe, but his hands were shaking badly. He had to keep stopping because he'd press in the wrong digit and the combination would die. Pappy pitied the guy. Fuck, maybe Black'd let him live. It wouldn't be the first time a pasty-faced middle-class white boy had been so scared he couldn't tell one black man from another.

Or maybe Black would threaten to come back and fuck him up for good if he didn't keep his mouth shut. Meaning the poor bastard'd be looking over his shoulder for the rest of his life.

He got the safe open.

"Nice. Now that's what I'm talkin' about," Black said, reaching in to lift out one of the small velvet-lined trays. There was a pouch on it. He untied the string and emptied the diamonds. He ran his hand through the stones, then picked one out and held it to the light. "Welcome to the big time." He hawked up a wad of phlegm and spat it out. All Pappy could think was: *There's the DNA evidence to tie the cracker to the crime.* "Stones. And all it took to get 'em was stones." Black laughed at his own joke.

"I'm with you, bro," said Von. "Let's grab this shit and split."

Ant and Gee started emptying trays of gems into

a black leather holdall before moving on to the display cases of rings and jewelry.

"Leave 'em. Too easy to trace. Besides, they're cheap shit. The money's in the stones. Ain't that so, Mr. H? Now these," Black continued, pulling out a tray of high-quality watches, "are sweet. I think I'll have me one of these." Black took a Rolex from the tray and slipped it on his wrist. He held it up for the others to admire. Pappy shook his head as he thought back to the "that's why white people call us niggers" speech Black gave in the car. Fucking hypocrite.

"Stop fucking around, man," Pappy said.

There was already more than enough in the holdall to give them new lives as kings if they wanted it. But that was where greed came into the equation. There was always more to be had.

"Let's get out of here," Pappy pushed. Every moment they were inside increased the risk of something going wrong.

"Chill, for fuck's sake, nigga," said Black. "There's no need to hurry. We got all the time in the world. No one's going to come busting in on us. Hell, you fixed the alarm so no one even knows that we're here, right, Pap?"

Pappy caught sight of the second guard glancing up at him, and knew instinctively that something was wrong.

The man seemed almost *pleased* that they were taking their time. But that wasn't it. The news that they had circumvented the alarm system didn't seem to bother him at all. The walkie-talkie crackled on his hip, asking for a sit-rep.

And then it hit him. It was every bit as obvious as Pappy's work-around, and every bit as lo-tech.

"Fuck!" Pappy snapped, pointing at the overweight guard with his flushed grin. "He's already called it in, man."

"What, with his hands tied behind his back?" Black laughed. "Who d'you think this motherfucker is, David Blaine?"

"No, you idiot. He radioed in before he came down the stairs. Forget the fucking alarm, he's already told 'em they've got intruders. We're fucked, bro. We've gotta get out of here, fast."

Black's expression shifted. It was subtle, but his eyes didn't lie. That tenuous control he had over his temper was failing. The rage started to build. Pappy looked at the others. They were playing statues. If something didn't happen, and happen fast, they were facing a reenactment of the bank job, and two dead men on his hands wasn't the way Pappy wanted to go down.

He turned to Black. "Come on, man."

"Shit!" Black shouted, punching the air in frustration. "Fuck shit fuck! Move it! Go! Now!"

But before they could move, Henderson spoke up: "What about my family?"

Black stared at him as though he were speaking Chinese. "What about them?"

"You promised if I helped you they wouldn't be hurt. When . . . when will you let them go?"

Black smiled cruelly. "Let them go? What makes you think they aren't already dead, you dumb fuck?"

Henderson whimpered, crumpling in on himself as though Black had just torn his spine out.

"I never fuckin' *had* them. Jeez, you stupid fuck." He shook his head.

"I don't understand . . ."

"He's telling you they're fine," Pappy said. "So let's just be cool and everyone goes home happy, okay?"

Henderson peered up at him, not fully believing. "They're safe?"

Pappy nodded. "They're safe."

"Good," the man said, starting to get to his feet. There was something different about him now. Gone was the timid little broker behind those wire-framed glasses. It wasn't courage he saw in Henderson's eyes. It was anger.

"How dare you?" It wasn't really a question.

A single shot answered Henderson's question as the Desert Eagle punched brutally through his chest. The impact hurled him from his feet and sent him sprawling back over the desk. A single red rose bloomed across his chest. There was nothing vaguely romantic about it. Henderson's head lolled to the side. There was an expression of surprise on his face. There was no life behind his eyes.

"Anyone else wanna ask a stupid question?" Black called out.

The two guards refused to make eye contact with him. They didn't say a word. Didn't move a muscle. Right then, in that moment, their lives hung in the balance.

Blood spread out around Henderson's body.

"Black!" Pappy yelled. "We have to go!"

Black's lips twitched into a mad, malicious grin. "You're right, Pap. You're always fuckin' right, nigga."

He grabbed a fistful of designer watches from the tray, not caring about their Swiss movements or how many jewels they had, and stuffed them into the holdall. He looked at the two men, one on his knees, the other still curled up on the ground, and asked the million-dollar question: "Can you gimme one good reason I shouldn't cap you motherfuckers?"

"Please . . ." the fat man said. "I've got a family. A wife. Kids. You don't have to do this. I won't tell anyone. I won't . . . Please."

"Not good enough," Black said, and double-tapped the trigger.

He stood over the last man, leaned in close, and pressed the still-hot barrel up against his temple. "Got any last words?"

Before he could beg for his life, Black pulled the trigger.

"Okay, now we get the fuck outta here, boys."

They could hear the sound of sirens in the distance.

EIGHT

VON HIT THE GAS, SLAMMING HIS FOOT TO THE FLOOR.
Tires screeched, burning rubber as they peeled
away from the parking lot. No one laughed. No one
hollered. No one said a fucking word despite the millions
in the holdall. It was as though a spell had been cast on
them. Maybe it was the adrenaline rush, the comedown
after the kill; maybe it was the ghost of the law in the air
all around them, sirens shrieking; maybe it was the fact
Black still held the Desert Eagle in his lap and his hand
was shaking and they knew he could just as easily shoot
them in the face as pat them on the back and say job
well done.

"Left here," Black barked. Von turned without slow-
ing. The van slewed through the turn as the tires lost
their traction, spitting gravel.

Pappy looked out between Black and Von. He could
feel Ant and Gee beside him. They were strung tighter
than a virgin's frilly pants.

"Right at the end." Black sniffed.

It was a single sniff—but it actually wasn't, Pappy

realized. Black had been sniffing the whole time. The fucker was loaded.

Pappy could have killed him there and then.

Maybe Von didn't know the streets, maybe Black hadn't told him where to go, but a smackhead shouting directions didn't instill confidence in him.

Searchlights speared the street up ahead. They roved wildly, crisscrossing over the rooftops and roads.

Now there was a helicopter up there looking for them.

"Fuck," Pappy said.

Black didn't seem to care. He acted like it was all part of the plan to get them killed. Suicide by cop? Not his style, surely.

Pappy thought about Tonya, and cursed himself for a fool. The things we do for women. Like get ourselves killed, he reflected bitterly.

The van swung to the right, mounting the sidewalk, then bumped back down onto the road, hitting one of the drains hard. "How much farther?" Von asked, getting control of the van again. He gassed the engine, taking it back up to top speed.

"Almost there," Black said. "Next left, into the alley."

Von slowed, barely, and scraped the side of the van against the wall as he turned into the narrow space. The headlights sent a rat scurrying from beneath one of the dumpsters along the side of the building. It disappeared into a hole. Pappy wished he could do the same.

The alley opened up into a vacant lot behind the buildings. It wasn't the kind of place where someone was likely to stumble upon them, but it wasn't safe from the police chopper's searchlight either. Something felt off.

Waiting in the lot was a single car. The interior light was on. Pappy saw Tonya behind the wheel.

She got out and walked around to pop the trunk.

At least this time there wouldn't be a body in it.

Black sniffed. "Let's make the switch. Leave the van here . . . Okay, dump the bags in the trunk."

There were no questions.

"Drop all the guns and the ski masks in there too," he added. "Ton and I'll dispose of them. We'll split here. You guys get back in the van. Pap, you drive from here. If you get stopped there will be nothing on you to link you to the robbery."

It almost sounded reasonable.

"We meet up to divvy the haul later?" Gee asked.

"Yeah," replied Black. "You know it, bro. Back to Sumner Houses for old times. One last gathering of the crew before we fuck off for pastures new. Toast our success."

They started back toward the van.

Tonya caught Pappy's eye.

She shook her head.

He held back.

He had no idea what she was trying to tell him, but as she shook her head again, more forcefully this time, he knew for sure something was wrong.

"Go," she whispered urgently. "Run. Please."

He didn't move.

As Gee, the last of the crew, climbed into the van, the gunshot told its own story.

The second shot came less than three seconds later.

Pappy heard Black's almost hysterical laughter, and a scream. He couldn't tell whether it was Von, Ant, or Gee. It didn't matter; soon enough none of them would be screaming.

Black was murdering three of his only friends in the world, and he was fucking laughing while doing it!

The next thing Pappy heard—after the thunderclap of the Desert Eagle died down—was a steady *drip, drip*.

It took him a moment to realize what it was: blood falling from the back of the van.

He glanced back toward Black's car, stunned. How could Tonya have come here? How could she have willingly been part of this? And make no mistake, she *was* part of it, even if she wasn't the one pulling the trigger. He hated her for it.

She was the reason he was here.

She was the reason he had just watched his friends slaughtered in the back of a stolen van.

And she was the reason Black was now pointing a gun at him.

NINE

"WHY?" PAPPY SAID.

"Why not, Pap?"

"That's not an answer."

Black shrugged. Black sniffed. Black raised the barrel of the gun, bringing it level with Pappy's heart.

"So what do you want me to say?"

"Try the fucking truth. You owe me that much."

"I don't owe you shit, Pap. One last job. Well, you got your wish. This is it. One last job. But you don't get to decide this shit. You don't get to call the shots. You're not the head fuckin' nigga in charge, Pap. That's me. I say when you get to walk. Fuck, son, I say *how* you get to go out, and I'm tellin' you it's in a body bag. You don't get to just fuckin' leave me, Pappy. Not after all we've been through. We were blood, man. Blood. And you stick a fuckin' knife in my back. Well, fuck you, you fuckin' fucker, your last job is done. So, now I'm done with you." His voice was getting louder, and shriller, the gun wavering as he held it out.

"Then do it," Pappy said. "Kill me. That's what you

want. Do it."

"You don't get to fuckin' tell me what to do, nigga. Not anymore. I decide. Me. You understand?"

"Fuck you, man. Just fuck you. What about Ton? You gonna kill her too? That part of your glorious plan?"

"Leave no nigga behind," Black said. There was no affection in it. This wasn't military loyalty. The threat was implicit; no one was going to be left to identify him.

"Well, maybe she got away in time," Pappy said. It was a petty victory, but he'd kept Black's attention on himself long enough for Tonya to creep into the alley. Now she was running.

He hoped she'd get away.

Black turned to look for her. Pappy had known he would. It was like those signs that said, *Beware: pickpockets operating in this area.* You check your wallet's still there, making it the perfect place for a pickpocket to work from. It's instinct. You can't fight it. Looking for Tonya was the same.

Pappy lunged forward, closing the distance between them in a heartbeat.

He was smaller than his old friend. In a straight fight he was only ever going to come off second best, so there was no way he was going to fight fair.

It was all about surprise.

Without it, Black was right, he was fucked.

Pappy made a grab for Black's arm, trying to get the gun.

He almost succeeded.

But Black thrashed back, wrestling himself away from Pappy's grip. The viciousness of the move meant he stumbled in the process. Pappy pushed forward, going with the stumble, and sent Black sprawling to the ground. It wasn't pretty but it was effective. Pappy was on him in a second, kicking and clawing as he tried desperately to pin his gun hand to the ground.

Black lashed out with his free hand, hammering his fist into the side of Pappy's head, which snapped back. Before he could bring it forward again, Black slammed another clubbing blow into his temple. And another. It was only because he was half-pinned down on the ground that meant he couldn't get all of his strength behind the blows; otherwise, Pappy would have been dead to rights.

Pappy had no plan. It was all instinctive now. Survival. There was no thought. He just had to move. Keep moving. Stay alive.

Those sirens were out there, but they might as well have been a million miles away. They weren't going to help.

The pain tore through him, intensifying with every punch Black landed.

He tried to fight back, to land one good solid blow of his own, but it was impossible without releasing the gun hand.

Black drove another fist into the side of his head. The huge golden signet ring he wore gouged out a chunk of flesh beneath Pappy's left eye. The impact lifted Pappy. It was all Black needed. He screamed. And used that rage to fuel a barrage of blows, yelling over and over, *"You don't get to fuckin' leave me! You don't get to fuckin' leave me!"* And then Pappy fell.

For a moment there was no pain.

The first bullet missed him. Black was shaking with rage and holding the Desert Eagle in that stupid execution pose, side-on.

Pappy lay on the ground looking up at the barrel and Black's rage-contorted face behind it.

The second bullet didn't miss.

There was no thunderclap.

Pappy didn't hear anything beyond his own heartbeat and the vague echoes of the movement around him. It seemed like an acid trip, but with incredible pain. Pappy felt dead, though he wasn't. The blood made his vision blurry, but he could see Black pouring gasoline all over the bodies in the back of the van. Then Black stood over Pappy's body and poured the gas on him, before dripping a trail of it that led outside. As Black moved off,

Pappy put together the little strength he had left to crawl away from the van. In his mind, far wasn't far enough once the fire started, and he was trying not to burn to death today. Then the pain and blood loss overcame Pap and he passed out. All that could be heard now was the crackle of the fire burning and then the roar of a car engine driving away.

Then the world turned cold. Pappy could smell gasoline, plus rubber and the burning flesh of his childhood friends.

And then it turned black as death and the law raced each other for him.

TEN

PAPPY HEARD VOICES.

He couldn't make out what they were saying.

Lights came and went.

Nothing was constant. Not the harsh ammonia that stung his nose. Not the deathly cold. Not the sirens or the machines.

He didn't know where he was.

Hell?

Or perhaps limbo, too much hate staining his soul for him to go up, redemption so close he couldn't go down?

He tried to open his eyes.

Voices cut across his brain. Excited.

He gave up and sank back into the black, denying them.

Let them wait.

The devil could take him later.

Time meant nothing. It didn't pass. It didn't stand still. It was irrelevant. Time was for another life.

There was something—a sound, like his heart but

not. Mechanical. Keeping him alive?

Concentrating on it meant that he wasn't thinking about death.

He saw Black in the black inside him. He wore a hoodie, the hood down over his face. Shadows swirled around his heels. He saw the silver of Black's Desert Eagle as he swept it around in a scything arc, and then a burst of light. He heard the cackle and rasp as his reaper claimed him.

You don't get to fuckin' leave me!

He felt the bullets hit again and again.

But this time he wanted to open his eyes.

This time he wanted to rip back Black's hood and stare death in its grim fucking rictus of a face and laugh.

Oh yes I do, he thought.

And took comfort in that thought.

But Black's reaper didn't leave him. He stalked him through the half-haze of sleep. Always with his hood down over his face. Always with his Desert Eagle instead of a scythe. It didn't matter what weapon death carried, Pappy thought, too tired to run.

Other sounds filtered through into the dark: the squeak of a wheel, rubber-soled shoes, the regular beep of some machine close to his left ear. But no matter how many more sounds came through, there was always that *click, click, click.*

He drifted in and out of black dreams that only got blacker.

Always the same thing. Always the muzzle. Always the bullet that killed him leaving the muzzle in slow motion.

He tried desperately to get out of the way—to change his death—but his muscles refused to react.

Black stood in front of him again. Head down, hands crossed at his waist. He had the Desert Eagle in his right hand, his left resting on the silver barrel.

Pappy still didn't move.

Black raised his head slowly.

You don't get to fuckin' leave me!

He stared into Black's eyes. There was no escaping the madness in them. He could see the back of the van reflected in them, the bodies of their friends lying there unmoving. Dead. All dead.

"Mr. Carter?"

That wasn't Black's voice.

The words didn't belong to death.

"Mr. Carter?"

Awareness stole unwillingly through him.

He felt something in his hand.

He tried to grip it.

A gloved finger lifted one of his eyelids.

A light was shone into his eye.

Now he couldn't close his eye. His body wouldn't obey him.

The finger released its grip. Pappy blinked away the tear it had caused. His vision was blurred. He couldn't focus on the woman leaning over him. It made her look like an angel in her scrubs.

He tried to move again. Pain filled his head. He choked down a wave of nausea.

"Pappy? Thank God."

He recognized the voice.

Did he already know God? Had she always been there in his life?

No.

This wasn't heaven.

It hurt too much.

He sank back into the pillow. He felt her hand in his. He tried to turn, just slightly, so he could look in her direction.

Tonya.

She was his guardian angel.

"You've been a *very* lucky man, Mr. Carter." He didn't feel it. "I don't know how much you remember yet, and if you're lucky, maybe you never will, but you were shot. Three times. One bullet shattered your collarbone, but did no real damage. The other passed through your thigh. Like I said, you were lucky. Both caused minor vascular wounds. An inch or two either side and we're talking major arteries. The third went through your lower abdomen, missing your spine by a fraction of an inch. EMTs on the scene saved your life. Unfortunately, your friends weren't so lucky."

"How long?"

"Almost two days," the doctor said. "We've been keeping you sedated to make sure that there were no other complications. I've told Ms. Deal here," he motioned at Tonya, "to go home and get some rest, but she refuses to listen to me. Perhaps you'll have better luck. You were extremely fortunate she was able to place the call to 911 so quickly. It made all the difference. A few minutes and, well, it doesn't bear thinking about, Mr. Carter. In these situations a few minutes is all it takes. Her quick thinking saved your life." She gave Tonya a sideways glance but no one said any more about it.

Pappy realized she'd made the call before he was shot. He'd heard EMT sirens, not the police.

"There's an officer who wants to speak to you when you feel up to answering his questions." She made a made a note on his records, then slipped them back into the holder at the foot of his bed. "If you need anything, just use that." She indicated a cord beside the bed. "It goes through to the nurse's station."

"Thanks, doc," Tonya said for him.

She nodded and left them alone.

"Black?" Pappy said when he was sure that they were alone.

It was only when he tried to speak that he realized just how dry his mouth was. Tonya noticed he was struggling and poured out a glass from a beaker of water.

She held the glass to his mouth and cradled his head as though he were a child. He couldn't keep his head up; there was no way he could have done this on his own.

But why was she there?

"He's gone," she said as she helped him sink back into the pillow. She wiped a dribble of water from the corner of his lips. "I was supposed to go with him."

"You knew that he was going to kill everyone?"

She shook her head. "No. You've got to believe me, Pappy. I had no idea. Not that he was capable of it." She sighed, and he did believe her. Despite everything she'd gone through at Black's hands she still saw the best in him. She was an addict, after all. Addicted to the abuse. Willing to excuse it. "I had a bad feeling, sure. I thought he might double-cross the other guys. But he swore to me he'd see you right before we skipped town."

"See me right into the ground," Pappy said. "You didn't guess what was coming? You drove that guy in . . . Then you drove the car back and waited for us."

"No. But when he popped the trunk . . ."

"What?"

"He told me he knew my secret."

"What secret? I don't understand, Ton."

"He said he knew I loved you more than I'd ever loved him."

Pappy looked at her. Properly. She wasn't lying. Maybe it would have been easier if she had been. Pappy shook his head. It made the world spin. "Why would he say that?"

"Because of the way he is. Because he's always convinced there's someone else. Because he never feels good enough. Because he thinks everyone's out to fuck him. Because I can talk to you, not him. Because the other night, he saw you touch my face." She held her hand to her cheek as though she could still feel the lingering trace of his palm.

"He tried to kill me because you were talking to me?"

"No. Because you were kind to me."

She couldn't look him in the eye.

Pappy had often thought Tonya stayed with Black because she was afraid of what might happen if she tried to leave. Now he knew for sure.

A tear fell onto his hand.

He didn't do tenderness easily. It wasn't his thing. But that didn't mean he was made of stone. He took her hand again. Squeezed it.

He thought about the others—Gee, Von, Ant—kids he'd known pretty much every day of his life, the only real friends he had. Gone. Ever since Sumner Houses they'd been the nearest thing to family for Pap.

Black had taken everything away from him.

"Where will you go?" he asked.

She shrugged. It was an infinitely expressive gesture—it spoke volumes, filled with heartache, shame, loss. She'd lost everything too.

That was the way Black worked. He'd isolated her from her real family, bringing her into the fold, and when he'd cut her off from all support, that's when the beatings started. Bitches liked a bastard. Nice guys came last. All that crap. It was all BS but it became some sort of fucked-up self-fulfilling prophecy. You got into the spiral and the only way was down. Maybe Ton'd be able to reach out to her folks and build bridges in time. But that'd be another life. Not here. Not now.

"Where's my stuff?"

"It's all in the cupboard." She nodded toward the bedside cabinet.

"Where will you go?" he asked again.

She shrugged once more.

"Take my keys. You can stay at my apartment."

"I can't."

"Course you can."

"I feel like I got you into this, Pappy. I wish . . . I just wish . . ." But she never said what it was she wished for.

His head was slowly beginning to clear. No doubt they'd pumped him full of morphine. Chances were, as soon as he was really able to think straight he'd start to feel the pain. He wasn't looking forward to it.

"I've only got a few days left on the lease," he said, "but the landlord said I can extend for a couple of months. Just need to give him a call. The number's next to the telephone. Give him a call. Explain. He's a good guy. There won't be any problem. Take some cash out of my wallet. Get some groceries."

She didn't move. "I . . . ." That was all she said.

"I don't blame you, Ton." And it was true. He didn't. She'd put herself at risk, and in the end, she'd run to save him. It wasn't exactly *Romeo and Juliet*, but then again that wasn't exactly a love story either. A seventeen-year-old getting jiggy with some thirteen-year-old girl? The only similarity was in the fact that people all around them wound up dead. So maybe that's *exactly* who they were. "Get some rest. I'm not going anywhere."

She didn't need to be told twice.

She was dead on her feet.

He could tell her to eat, rest, but he couldn't make her.

And yet even just thinking about sleep was enough to make his eyelids close.

And in his dreams Tonya lay curled up next to him.

ELEVEN

WHEN PAPPY WOKE HE FELT MORE ALIVE.

Or a little less dead.

It was difficult to say.

He kept his eyes closed for a moment. He lay there listening for the sounds that had kept him going during the drug-induced coma. The bleep of the monitor had gone. He could still hear the squeak of a trolley wheel, the sound of rubber-soled shoes. But where was the other sound? He tried to find it. One sound. One voice. That steady *click, click, click*.

He listened hard, trying to block everything else out.

There it was.

He opened his eyes, straining toward the sound. The second hand of a large white clock on the wall. Maybe time hadn't been so meaningless after all. He was alive and the one thing that had kept him going was the ticking of a fucking clock. It hurt to laugh.

Tonya wasn't there.

But the chair she'd been sitting in wasn't empty.

A middle-aged man sat in it reading a newspaper. "Still in the land of the living then?"

"Doesn't look like it."

"Ah, where would this be then? Hell? You a good Christian boy, Patrick?"

"You a cop?"

"Bright boy."

They were interrupted by a pretty nurse who bustled into the room and adjusted his pillows without even acknowledging the man in the chair. "Hello, Mr. Carter," she said, all smiles. "How are you feeling?"

"Like I've been shot."

He winced as she angled him up the bed and busied herself with the drip.

"Well, I wonder why that is." She raised an eyebrow. "The good news is we should be able to get the drips removed once the doctor has taken a look at you. Might even get you out of here soon. Is there anyone at home to help you?"

"You're sending me home?"

"Not right this minute." She smiled. "But soon enough. As long as there's someone at home to look after you."

"Yeah, I've got someone to help out," he said. Did he really?

The police officer waited until the nurse started to

leave. He watched her ass with admiration as she walked away. "So, Patrick, are you going to tell me what the fuck happened out there? I've got a lot of questions. I think you might have some answers."

"You're looking for Alex Trebek—he's in the room next door," Pappy said. "I don't have any answers."

"Wise guy, huh?"

"You think if I was wise I'd have wound up getting shot?"

"Good point. So, how about you talk me through what happened?"

"Not a lot to tell. I heard some trouble going down. I went to take a look. Curiosity almost killed this fucking cat. That's it, the big story."

The cop wasn't buying it. What else could he say?

"So, you're trying to tell me you weren't part of the crew that got killed out there? You just *happened* to walk into the middle of a massacre involving a bunch of your friends? Now, I may look like a fucking cunt to you, but do me a favor, don't treat me like one. You know that's not true, I know it's not true. So cut the bullshit, Patrick. What happened out there?"

"I ain't done nothing except get myself shot."

"Okay, let's try this again. You know Maurice Black?"

There was no point in denying it, they had been at

school together, lived side by side in Sumner Houses—
the cop knew that, it was all public record shit. Forensics would find his prints and DNA all over Black's
crib.

"Sure, I know Black."

"Drinking buddies?"

"Drinking, fucking, we're tight, you know how it is.
So, what's he done that's got you all excited?"

The policeman laughed. He sounded genuinely
amused. Maybe Pappy had a career in stand-up waiting
for him when he got out of here. "Okay, if you want to
play it that way, that's what we'll do. Your friend Maurice
Black and some of his like-minded friends committed a
robbery. It didn't go all that well from what we can tell."

"Really?"

"Let's just say there was a falling out amongst
thieves. Black shot the rest of his crew. Nice boy, your
fuck buddy."

Pappy didn't blink an eye. "That's what I walked in
on then."

The man's laugh was reduced to a wry smile. "Of
course you did."

"You seem to know what's the what, so what exactly
do you think I can do for you?"

"Let's just say—for argument's sake—that *you* were
part of the crew that hit the jewelry depot, and so was

that pretty little thug who's been sitting vigil over your bedside."

"Tonya?"

"Ah, right, yes, Tonya Deal, Maurice's *girlfriend*, right?"

"That's right."

"Now, why would Maurice's girlfriend be sitting by your bed worrying her pretty little ass off when her man was the one who put three bullets in you? That's a question I'd love to hear the answer to."

"It's like a motherfucking riddle or something," Pappy said.

"Let me tell you what I think's about to happen. I think you're about to give her an alibi. And I think you're full of shit. So save your breath. I *know* you were part of that robbery."

"Do you now? Because there's CCTV footage?"

They both knew there was no footage.

"Well, Patrick, here's the thing: I know you were there, and I can place you at the scene. You might have sorted out the CCTV for one set of cameras, but you'll be amazed what speed cameras capture at stoplights. So, given I know you were in the van on the way to the robbery, and I know you were found in a pool of blood with your crew who committed the robbery, and I know that the bullets they pulled out of you and your friends match

the ones that killed the jewelry depot's security guards
. . . Add that to the security footage we've pulled from
a failed robbery attempt on a bank last week in which
Maurice's face is clearly shown, and another man died,
I'd say reasonable doubt's going to be a bitch for any
lawyer. At the very least you'd be looking at is accessory
to murder. Third strike and you're out, Patrick, you know
the deal. Let's just go with the flow for a while. I think
it's safe to assume that aside from three extra bullets, you
haven't profited from the theft, so I'm willing to believe
all of the killings were down to Maurice Black, and that
you and Miss Deal were innocent bystanders caught up
in his killing spree. If you're willing to help us."

"What makes you think I'd be able to help even if I
wanted to?"

"You're a friend of his. You've known each other for
a long time. People take. Maybe you've got an idea of
where he might have gone? Some dream? Maybe he always hankered for Detroit, say? No, that was you, wasn't
it? So what about Maurice?"

"You tried the crib?"

"If you mean that crack house he's been living in—
yes, we've paid it a visit. Cleaned out. My guess—and
believe me, I'm a really fucking good guesser when it
comes to this stuff, Patrick—he's headed straight out
of town. I'm not interested in you, Patrick. Getting this

fucker off the street is more important than sending his foot soldier down. Help me find him and I'll stop trying to find ways of connecting you and your young lady to the whole fucking mess."

Pappy met his gaze. "If I think of anything I'll let you know."

"And you think that'll be enough, do you, son? Fob me off with a platitude? I thought we'd done away with that whole dumb-white-cunt crap."

The man got up from his chair and perched himself on the side of the bed. He was a little too close to Pappy's injured leg for comfort. As he sat down the mattress shifted slightly. Pappy felt the pain shoot from the bullet wound up his leg, all the way into his ball sack. He clenched his jaw, refusing to cry out.

"That's gotta hurt," the cop said sympathetically. "Now, I don't want to have to drag you down to the station. And the last thing I want's a good kid like you dying on me in custody—way too much fucking paperwork—but don't think that means I'm just gonna walk out of here and let you and Ms. Deal play happy fucking family. I've seen enough domestic violence cases to know where those bruises on her face came from. You've got nothing to gain by protecting Maurice now. Remember, he tried to kill you. You're not bros, or homies, or whatever the fuck it is you call yourselves. If I were a gambling man

I'd put it all on black, so to speak. Your boy is going to come back to finish what he started back there. No loose ends. You pair, you're loose ends."

The detective placed a card on the cabinet.

He collected his newspaper and stood up again.

The mattress shifted under the redistributed weight and Pappy stiffened every muscle against the lancing pain.

"I'll come by tomorrow, see if you've remembered anything. Have a nice day, Patrick."

TWELVE

TONYA CAME BACK AFTER THE DOCTOR HAD DONE HER ROUNDS. The drip had been removed and they'd changed his dressings.

It had all been polite enough, but they'd basically said sucks to be you, there's nothing we can do for you now that rest won't do, and it's not like you're Mr. Blue Cross. He guessed Obamacare hadn't made it all the way down to his kind just yet. They gave him some Tylenol/codeine hybrid, to take as needed, assuring him that the mix would basically be morphine when it hit his system, and an appointment to come back to have his dressings changed again.

"The pins in your shoulder'll set off metal detectors, so try not to upset the TSA guys next time you fly, okay?"

He smiled at the joke, but getting through airport security was the least of his worries.

Tonya arrived a few minutes later. His worries didn't seem quite so bad for a few minutes.

"You're looking better today," she said, placing a

bag next to the bed. It was full of fresh clothes. "Almost handsome."

"Only almost? I guess being shot is like being hit with the ugly stick, eh? So, how about it: you, me, outta here? I'm about done with being the sick guy."

She didn't argue with him.

When the nurse returned, Tonya gave her all the reassurances she needed, and the doctor agreed to discharge him, giving Tonya a list of instructions while the nurse helped Pappy into his clothes.

"How did you get here?" Pappy asked her as she wheeled him toward the doors. The hospital wouldn't let him walk out. They wouldn't let him keep the wheelchair either. It was all slightly comic. The orderly helped him out of the chair and he stepped into the fresh air for the first time in what felt like forever.

"You take it easy, sir," the orderly suggested, but he was already on his way back inside before Pappy could say thanks.

"Von's car," Tonya said. "Didn't think he'd mind, all things considered. Y'know? He leaves—*used* to leave— a spare key in a magnetic box underneath the driver's side door. Thought he was being clever. Like any nigga'd want to steal that heap of crap."

THIRTEEN

H E FELT EVERY JERK AND BOUNCE THROUGH THE SHOT SUSPENSION AS SHE drove to his apartment.

The car had seen better days. And then it had seen worse days. Now it was barely seeing any days at all. There was a bullet hole in the rear driver's side door. Ton was right; it was hard to imagine anyone wanting to steal it. Von might as well have left the keys in the ignition with a sign saying, *Try your luck.*

They made small talk.

The smaller the talk the better.

They didn't want to talk about any of the big stuff they'd been through.

She'd stocked the refrigerator.

She'd okay'd it with the landlord, who had been happy to give Pappy as much time as he needed to get back on his feet.

She'd cleaned up, unpacking some of the boxes.

She'd made it feel like a home again, even if it was only temporary.

His computer gear was untouched.

Walking hurt. Sitting down hurt.

He crunched a couple of painkillers while she brewed strong black coffee.

Pappy looked at the computer screen.

He'd need to get working if he was going to deal with Black's betrayal. He had an idea where the fucker might have run to, but he wasn't about to share that with Mr. Law Enforcement. That wasn't how you dealt with betrayal where he came from. He had an idea, but Tonya had to *know*.

"Where's he gone, Ton?" Pappy asked, when she came back with the hot coffee. He sank into the armchair.

She shrugged her shoulders. It wasn't exactly the most credible denial. Maybe she didn't know. Or maybe she was still frightened of Black. The answer behind door number two was far more believable.

"Okay, how about this? I'll tell you where he's gone and you can tell me if I am wrong. Miami," Pappy said. Black had mentioned the place often enough, like it was his holy grail, his dream destination.

"I guess so, but he didn't say," she replied. It was as close a confirmation as she was likely to give. "You can't go looking for him, Pappy. He'll kill you this time."

"Oh, I ain't going *now*. But the cops aren't gonna ignore all those bodies, and as soon as he knows I'm still alive he'll be back."

"Why would he risk it? He's got everything he ever wanted and there's nothing here for him."

"He'll be back because that's who he is. Either para-noia, 'coz he can't keep living looking over his shoulder, or greed, because we both know no amount of millions are enough for him. He'll run out of money. Doesn't matter how much he gets for the diamonds, he'll blow through it, and when he does he'll come home. He doesn't belong there. You can take the boy outta Sum-ner Houses, but you can't take Sumner Houses outta the boy. I'm just gonna find him before he finds me. Then I'm gonna take what's mine."

"You've already got what's yours, if you want it," Tonya said.

He smiled. It only hurt when he laughed.

"How will you find him?" she asked. "We can't just go to Miami and start asking around."

That was true. "We've got this"—he motioned at his computer gear—"my magic wand." He was hoping he knew enough to be able to track Black down. People didn't just disappear, even newly rich niggas like Black. "Might need you to help me though."

"Maybe I can do more than help," she said. For a moment it sounded overtly sexual. It wasn't. She opened her bag. She'd already cleaned out the crib, grabbing anything remotely financial, thinking it might leave some sort of trail. It wasn't as though he'd left a ton of credit card slips or bank statements lying around, but all it would take was one number. One lead. She pulled out a fistful of papers. Black, Pappy, and the whole crew had real licenses and passports in different names. A female they all knew from Sumner Projects worked in the Department of Motor Vehicles. Four hundred dollars per. Black alone had at least four different aliases. All official and all clean names.

Pappy fired up the computer to get to work. While he was waiting for it to boot up he retrieved the gun he kept under the mattress. Just because he thought Black was already in Miami didn't mean that's where he really was.

FOURTEEN

I T TOOK THEM THREE DAYS TO TRACK HIM DOWN.

Three days of staring at the computer screen.

Three days of false leads and dead ends.

Three days of frustration.

Three days of ever-decreasing hope.

And then a single second of luck.

Pappy had hoped that he'd find some sort of bill of sale for a new car. Maybe a phone number going into a new ocean-view apartment or a lease agreement. Something. Fuck, even a goddamn boat or harbor charges. They were all part of Black's big Miami dream.

But it was none of these that gave them the break.

The statements and letters in all the different aliases Tonya had retrieved from Black's place had yielded enough information for him to access his bank details, not that Black had ever used the online banking system—but he had been very helpful and written his password on the letter they had mailed out with the log-in details: *MIAMIBEACH*. The fact that he hadn't destroyed the document or taken it with him meant he didn't care about it. Maybe he'd never even used the account.

There was only one way of finding out.

Thirty seconds later Pappy had access to his records.

He tabbed through the statements. It didn't take a genius to realize Black had been using the account to try to build up his getaway stash. The balance increased in irregular increments, and Pap was sure that if he ran the dates against their robberies he'd see some sort of link.

There had been no deposits since the jewelry depot.

Pappy read between the lines: he'd not converted the proceeds to cash. But then he found the kicker: the last withdrawal—emptying the account—had been from an ATM in Miami.

This was his proof.

The withdrawal had been yesterday.

Pappy checked the personal details on the account and could not believe what he was seeing. Black might as well have thought he was living in an episode of *Miami Vice*, pre-computers, because he was fucking clueless when it came to how they worked, what sort of information they stored, and how anyone with an Internet connection and a bit of stubbornness could get to it.

He'd given the bank his new address.

Pappy shook his head.

They were going to have to act quickly if they

wanted to get to him before the police—because there was no way they weren't monitoring his accounts, dumb fucker. This wasn't state, this was FBI shit. All those IDs with different names didn't matter cause of three words: *face-recognition technology*. Homicide detectives were the least of their worries. It was time to pick up the pace. Even if they didn't stop for gas, piss, food, and sleep, and traffic was good all the way, it'd take damn near twenty-four hours to drive there. He was in no shape for such a long haul, meaning they'd need to rest up, break the journey into stages, and that meant days.

They didn't have days.

They would have to fly.

FIFTEEN

PAPPY WAS GLAD THAT THE NURSE HAD WARNED HIM ABOUT THE METAL PINS setting off scanners.

The TSA and Homeland Security guys had been more than a little cautious when they'd rolled up, but they'd waved him through eventually.

They had enough cash to hire a car for a couple of days, and rent a room for a night. Then they'd be cleaned out. With luck that'd be longer than they needed. Any longer and they'd be beaten to the punch by Miami-Dade PD or the feds.

The address they had was a sleaze-pit of a motel not far from the airport.

It was one of those no-questions-asked, by-the-hour places where cash was king, queen, and gimp all rolled into one amenable package.

Money had been spent to bring it into the twenty-first century with its vibrating mattresses, vending machines, and Wi-Fi connection, just not a lot.

For some reason it felt like Black was planning on staying here for a while.

It didn't make sense.

He had a fortune, and not a small one.

He must have made the contacts to cash it in. Sure, he wouldn't get face value for the diamonds, and Pappy had no idea how much their haul was really worth, but it had to be seven figures. Had to be. Even if you were bent over and fucked royally by the buyers.

Black's car stood by itself in the parking lot. There were half a dozen other cars in different rows.

It was calling out to the cops to come and get him.

Pappy shook his head. He couldn't believe how stupid the guy had become. But then he remembered just how much he'd changed.

Did he think he was suddenly untouchable? Above the law? Had the coke worn away the last vestiges of his self-defense mechanisms?

Pappy could not be sure, but Black wouldn't survive long if he kept on like this. New car, new home, new name were the minimum requirements. A shithole of a motel room wasn't even close.

"What do we do now?" Tonya asked.

"End it," Pappy said. It wasn't a great answer, but it was an answer. They hadn't talked about what they'd do if they found him—probably because he'd not actually believed they would find him. Pappy didn't have his gun. It wasn't like he had a carry permit for it, so he could hardly fill in the TSA forms and bring it with him on the plane, and even with the pins he wasn't going to try and smuggle it through security. Getting caught would have brought on a world of hurt.

Now that they were here, he didn't know what he was going to do.

Just confront him?

A few phone calls to people who owed him favors might lead to a chain that would eventually get him a piece, but when too many people knew you were looking for a gun, and knew you'd been shot, it wouldn't be hard for someone to put two-and-two together. The news that he was out looking for Black would get back to the cops. Or to Black. He didn't want either of them knowing until the last possible moment.

It could be the difference between walking away from this and not.

Pappy fished his cell out of his pocket and called the number on the motel's sign.

The phone was answered by a woman. She sounded as though she was talking around a cigarette or a small cock. Either was possible, he supposed, given the place. He explained that he thought a friend of his was staying there. He gave Black's name and asked if she could put him through to his room. She munched some more dick and put him through.

Black answered on the third ring. "Yo?"

"'Sup," Pappy said.

"Who the fuck's this?"

"Ghost of Christmas past."

There was silence on the line for a moment.

"Fuck off."

Pappy saw movement in a car parked in the next row and the driver pressed a finger to an earpiece.

He hung up without another word.

"We've got company," he told Tonya.

He nodded toward the car. They could barely make out its two occupants.

"Police?" she asked.

Pappy nodded. It changed things. He wasn't sure how much, but there was no way around the fact they couldn't just walk up to Black's room and knock on the door now.

The woman hadn't said what room he was in. She didn't need to. The cops were eyeballing one of two doors, either six or seven, it was hard to say which one for sure. The curtains to both were closed.

The door to number six opened and a young couple stepped out.

"Number seven it is," he said, watching the couple make their way to a small red sedan. "Drive around the other side. I've got an idea."

She pulled away from the curb, taking the car slowly around the side of the building. They drove past the cops. Neither man turned to look at them. Like fixated game show contestants they were all about what was behind door number seven.

Room number seventeen backed directly onto number seven.

He allowed himself a faint smile.

"Ton, go to reception, see if seventeen's free." He handed her a wad of crumpled bills. She nodded and clambered out of the car. He watched her make her way to the front of the building.

Because they'd known each other forever, he'd always somehow thought of her as just a girl. She wasn't a girl. She was every inch a woman. What was it the cop had called her? A pretty thug. Yeah. She was pretty. He couldn't remember ever thinking that way before. Maybe when this was done . . . maybe they were both due a fresh start? Could you ever wipe the slate clean? Erase the past? They'd been through more than most couples. Maybe that'd give them a bond?

Or maybe he was out of his fucking mind on pain meds? He laughed at that. It was a laugh that was dangerously close to being out of control. He couldn't afford that. He needed to get a grip. Cold and rational, that was what he needed to be.

He sat in the car, flexing the fingers on his bad arm. There was no strength in them. He sent out a silent prayer to whoever looked after girls like Tonya, willing them to keep Black away from the window long enough for her to come back to him. They must have been listening: she came around the corner with the key dangling from one finger.

He climbed out of the car and followed her to the door.

"Any problems?"

"Nope. They had someone due to arrive later, but I told the woman that we spent our wedding night in seventeen and wanted to recapture the romance."

"What she did say to that?"

"If he's so romantic, how come the little shit sent you to book the room, honey?" Tonya chuckled as she opened the door.

Pappy tried not to laugh too loudly.

She placed a finger to her lips and nodded to the far end of the room, meaning Black was on the other side of that paper-thin wall. For all they knew, he would be able to hear every single word they said from now on. He nodded and went inside. She followed him in and closed the door behind them.

Pappy peered around the room.

It was dominated by a double bed with a coin slot on the headboard.

He sat down and felt the springs give a little beneath his ass.

He felt dead on his feet.

"You need to get some rest," Tonya said. She didn't have to read his mind, it was written all over his face.

She helped him out of his jacket—which was far too warm for the Miami heat—and eased him onto the bed.

When he woke the sun had set and Tonya was asleep in her bra and panties, curled up as close to him as she could be.

He didn't want to move in case he woke her. He looked at her creamy skin. It was flawless in the moonlight save for a dark-purple bruise around her ribs. He hated Black in that moment more than he had hated anyone in his life. He stroked a strand of hair away from her face. She opened her eyes sleepily but obviously wasn't awake.

Something about the cops out in the parking lot worried away at the back of his mind. Why were they sitting in their car watching rather than picking Black up?

Local law enforcement should have brought him in, surely? They'd wait for backup, but that didn't mean they'd stake out the motel. It wasn't like they'd wait for the old guy who'd visited Pappy in the hospital to fly down to make the arrest personally, would they?

Only one thing made sense: they were going to use Black to catch someone bigger.

Bigger than eight murders.

Bigger than millions of dollars worth of stolen gems.

That realization scared Pappy.

What the fuck had Black gotten himself mixed up in?

He lay there gazing at the spiral galaxy stippled into the plaster on the ceiling, watching the fan turn lazily. It rocked on every second revolution, like whatever screws held it in place were slowly coming undone. The neon light from the vacancy sign lit the room. It wasn't exactly paradise, but with Tonya beside him it might as well have been.

Pappy managed to move her hand so he could slide off the bed without waking her.

He crept across to their one bag, and fished out the pills. He crunched a handful of them. The pain was nowhere near as bad as it had been only a couple of days ago, but he was still a long way from fully healed. It'd be a month or more, for sure. And he could well be walking with a limp for the rest of his life.

Tonya stirred again.

He would have killed to be able to just get back into that bed, touch her cheek the way he had done in Black's crib. He thought about reaching down to unclasp her bra, and slipping off her panties, and what it would feel like to be inside her. And then forced himself to stop. Thinking like that would get him killed.

SIXTEEN

AIN'T ASKING AGAIN. WHO THE FUCK IS THIS?" BLACK SAID DOWN THE LINE.

Pappy smiled. For once he felt like he was in control. He leaned against the cinder-block wall at the end of the lot, glancing back at the building, the doors to six and seven, and the cars in between. No one could see him. Not unless they had eyes in the back of their head.

"You killed me once. Now it's my turn."

"Pap? That you, man? Tell me it's you, you motherfucker. My god, it's good to hear your voice, nigga."

"You killed Pappy, *Maurice*," he said, drawing it out real slow. *More reese*, like the pieces. "Three bullets, *pop, pop, pop*."

"But you survived, dog. I know your fuckin' voice, Pap. No bullet can take a nigga down, eh?"

"Can't kill a dead man."

"Stop fuckin' with me, Pap. Where you at?" Not *What do you want?*

"Close by."

"Stop fuckin' with me, Pap. I'm serious."

"Riddle me this, *Maurice* . . . How'd I know where you were staying?"

"What the fuck d'you want, ghost?"

"My share."

"That it? You came all this fucking way back from the dead for your lousy fucking *share*? You're killin' me, Pap."

"That's the plan."

Black sniffed. "Seems to me you took my bitch. I'd say that makes us even. In other words, go fuck yourself, son."

"She's not a bitch, Maurice, and I didn't *take* her. You left her behind."

"You make it sound like the fuckin' rapture, Pap. I didn't fuckin' leave her behind. That ain't how I see it. You took her from me. You always were a weasely little cunt. Should have known you'd stick your fuckin' knife in my back. Or your dick in my woman. Ain't no way to treat a brother."

"We're not brothers, Maurice." He liked saying that name. It was a little disrespect, like a boxer leading with an insistent jab, just poking away, hitting the same bruised ego over and over again. "And to be honest, I don't give a fuck how you *see* it. You were beating on your woman, you put bullets in your crew—you ask me, you deserve everything coming to you."

"You fucked her, dude. I know you did. Ain't no point lying to me, Pap. She told me. You telling me that bitch is a liar on top of everything else? Sure, why not? She's a lying whore."

"Don't talk about her like that. Don't even say her fucking name." Another jab.

"She really did a fuckin' number on you, didn't she, bro? And to think I used to like you. Just fuck off, Pap. You're out of your depth, son."

"You worried 'bout the wrong shit, Maurice. I want what's mine. Give me that and I'll walk away." Jab.

"Fuckin' crack head. Nigga, you're out of your mind."

"That your final word?"

"You ain't gettin' a red fuckin' cent outta me, Pap."

"Doesn't work for me. You wanna come see me, big man? Sort this out face to face?"

"Don't make me do this, Pappy. We used to be friends . . ."

"Don't make you do . . . da fuck else you gone do to me? You already put three bullets in me. You killed all of us and then set us on fire. Remember? Fuck your kind of friendship, Maurice." Jab. "I'll be near the lifeguard seats in half an hour. Don't be a fucking fag, Maurice. Be there. I'll be waiting."

Pappy hung up before Black had the chance to respond. He wanted him angry; he wanted him to go charging straight out of the motel room. He wanted to put the fear of God into him.

He was not disappointed.

Less than sixty seconds later Black was out of the door and marching to his car. Another thirty seconds and he was in it and away, burning rubber. The undercover cops were twenty seconds behind him. In less than two minutes from killing the call he'd emptied the lot and sent the cops off on a wild goose chase. Not bad for one phone call. That was probably why the whole myth of the one phone call had kicked off. With one phone call you could change the world, so surely you could spring yourself out of jail.

Pappy smiled. He couldn't remember where he'd heard that about the one phone call being a lie, probably in a Starbucks when one of those wannabe screenwriters was banging on about it. The shit you heard in those places was unreal.

He waited until he was sure both vehicles were out on the turnpike, then called Tonya in room seventeen. She didn't answer. She wasn't meant to. He watched the door of number seven and started to count slowly, marking the time.

It took nine minutes for Tonya to unscrew the cover on the air-conditioning vent and wriggle through. He couldn't have done it if his life depended on it, but she was lithe enough to squirm through and drop to the floor without breaking half the bones in her body. She turned the light on. Pappy breathed out a huge sigh of relief. He hadn't realized he was holding his breath. The door was opened by a dust-streaked Tonya.

They had an hour, maybe less. It depended on how impatient Black was when he got to the beach and couldn't find Pappy.

Black had been traveling light. There were two changes of clothes in the closet and they both looked like they needed laundering already. Pappy was hoping that Black hiding out in this shithole meant he hadn't been able to off-load the diamonds yet. Which meant they had to be in here. Black wouldn't have taken them down to the beach, just in case something went wrong. So they had to be hidden here somewhere.

Or not.

No amount of searching turned them up.

"We've got to think like him," Tonya said after ten minutes wasted going through the same empty drawers, feeling around at the back just in case they'd missed something the first time. They peered down the backs of the few pieces of furniture, angling the dresser away from the wall far enough to see there was nothing behind it. "He's paranoid. He's probably jacked up on some shit. Where'd he hide the stones?"

Pappy was getting angry with himself. He kept checking the clock on the wall. The only thing he found was Black's Desert Eagle tucked beneath his pillow.

Black wouldn't have gone off without a piece—but this was the gun that had put down Ant and Von and Gee. Pappy held it carefully in both hands, like it might rear up and strike him.

Symmetry.

There was something poetic about finding the Desert Eagle here.

If he believed in fate he'd have said it was telling him there was a certain kind of justice here: the chance to kill Black with the same gun he'd used to kill the Sumner Houses crew.

Let the cops worry about forensics matching the bullets to all the crimes.

Pappy tucked the Desert Eagle into the back of his jeans and went to check out the bathroom.

He scanned the medicine cupboard. The shelves were empty. There was a single bottle of cheap shampoo on the tub. He was about to walk out when he noticed scratches on the wall beside the bath. He knelt down and examined them. The same white scratches were on the enamel bath panel. "Well, what have we got here then?" Pappy said, working the panel free.

It was the black leather holdall.

But there were no jewels inside.

There was a well-wrapped package of what must have been at least two keys of coke and a plastic supermarket bag of fifty-dollar bills.

"I don't believe it," Tonya said behind him. "He's dealing? He's traded the diamonds for dope?"

"Looks like it. Because that's a lot of coke for the new boy in town to move."

"What the fuck does he think he's doing?"

"He's playing the part. King of fuckin' New York. He always loved that damn film." Pappy shook his head.

They heard the sound of a car pulling into the lot. Pappy killed the light. He could only hope that no one had noticed it.

He helped Tonya wriggle back up into vent and pushed the bag of bills in after her, then, working fast, he replaced the grille.

He hid in the bathroom.

He didn't have time to replace the panel before he heard the key being pushed into the lock.

Black slammed the door behind him. He wasn't happy. That pleased Pappy. He listened carefully as Black emptied his pockets and dropped his gun down on the dresser. He kicked out at the chair before dropping on the bed. Pappy could picture it all by piecing the sounds together.

He waited.

"This is room seven," Black snarled, obviously speaking into the telephone. "Has anyone called in the last half an hour?"

He slammed the receiver down a couple of seconds later.

Jab.

Jab.

Time for the knockout.

Pappy pulled the door open slowly. It didn't make a sound. He saw Black lying on the bed, rubbing his hands over his face. Pappy didn't move. He stood there, watching, waiting.

Then Black saw him.

It was almost comical. He jerked back in the bed like he'd been shot. He scrambled about for a second as though he'd expected someone else, and then fell back laughing.

"What the fuck are you doing here, Pap? I didn't order turndown service." He cast a glance toward the gun he had put on the dressing table, but didn't make a move for it.

"Like I told you on the phone, Maurice, I'm here for what's owed me."

"Will you stop calling me that fuckin' name, Pappy. I ain't no fuckin' Maurice."

Jab.

"Oh, that's right, nigga. You're Black, right? Fucking Black, color of death."

"Fuck you, Pap. That's some prejudice shit."

"Time to pay up, Maurice."

"I told you, nigga, you're shit outta luck. There ain't no fuckin' money here, and no fuckin' stones. It's done, over."

"Really? You expect me to believe that?"

"It's the fuckin' truth, man."

He was beginning to know how that cop had felt questioning him in the hospital. Maurice Black wasn't a good liar. He sniffed.

"So what about the bag under the tub?" Pappy asked.

The look of surprise was priceless.

Black shifted on the bed. His hand snaked under the pillow, searching for the gun that wasn't there.

"Lost something?" Pappy winced as he reached around the back of his jeans for the Desert Eagle stuffed in the waistband. He leveled it at Black. "This is this the gun you tried to kill me with, isn't it? The one you killed Von and Gee and Ant with?"

Black pushed himself farther back up the bed, like he was trying to climb the wall. There was no way out of the shitty little motel room. It wasn't the kind of place any kind of king wanted to die. But Black wasn't a king. He scrambled back, his feet kicking up the grimy cotton sheets. He knew what was going to happen next and there was nothing he could do to stop it.

"Take it," he said. "Take it all. It's yours, Pap. For old times. Sumner Houses, bro. Take it. You and Ton, go make a new life, make babies. My blessing, nigga. No hard feelings."

"Plenty of hard feelings, Maurice," Pappy shot back. "It's over. Time for those last words. Some sparkling wit. Something to say you were here, that your place among us was worthwhile. You only get one shot, make it good." He reached inside the bathroom and pulled out one of the folded towels. He wrapped it around the gun like a cheap silencer and stepped closer. He didn't want the two men who were no doubt back sitting vigil outside to hear, and he didn't want to miss either.

Pappy had never seen Black like this; he was always the one in control, the one pointing the gun, not the man afraid for his life. Role reversal was a bitch. Pappy kept expecting him to make a desperate lunge for the gun. It would have been so much easier to kill him if he did. It would become self-defense. He could rationalize that.

Black didn't move. All he could do was press himself up against the wall and beg.

"I didn't want to kill you, bro. I didn't know what I

was doing. It was the coke. Fucked with my head, man. You gotta believe me. It was that bitch, Ton, always going on at me. Driving me mad. Gotta have money. Nothing I ever did was good enough. Gotta have more. Always fuckin' more." Black trotted out every excuse under the sun. But he didn't once say sorry. And he didn't once offer the truth, the real truth: he had done it because he could, because he wanted to, because he enjoyed it. Because he couldn't let Pappy walk away.

Not that it would have saved him.

"You can't do this to me," Black said. "Not after everything we've been through, bro. We're blood."

"You did it to me."

"Nah, man, that was different."

"How?"

"I was in charge. I was the head nigga. You were my men. My team. I gave the orders, you did what I said. That's just the way that shit was. You were mine." The words were tumbling out of his mouth now. Pappy saw tears welling up in his eyes. He was a beaten man, a broken man.

Pappy knew that he could have walked away. He'd won. Black wasn't in charge. Pap was the head nigga now. Only he didn't have a crew. Truth was, he didn't want one either. He was done with that life. He could have walked away with the drugs, the cash, and the last of the diamonds, and left Black alive; it was over. Black wouldn't have come looking for him. He wouldn't have had a clue how to find him. But that was not what he wanted.

The cash in the bag would pay for a new life. He didn't need the coke. And the diamonds were covered in his friends' blood. The only thing he *wanted* was revenge.

Taking everything from Black, leaving him a broken man, wasn't enough.

"She did this to us," Black pleaded, "she came between us. Fucked with our heads. I believe you, man. You never touched her. She lied." It was a last desperate cry for mercy. It didn't bring him clemency. "You're my boy, Pap. You and me. Sumner Houses. You and me against the world."

Pappy pulled the trigger.

Twice, three times, one for each bullet Black had pumped into him, completing the cycle.

Symmetry.

The first shot hit Black square in the chest. A red bloom spread quickly across his white vest. The second, aimed slowly, deliberately, destroyed his cock. It was for Tonya. For every time he'd hit her. Every time he'd abused her. The third struck Black in the face, leaving nothing to chance.

"I guess I do get to leave you after all," Pappy said to the dead man.

The towels had muffled the sound of the gun, but he couldn't be sure how well.

He had to move fast.

He pulled the metal grille away from the air vent again. "Ton?" he called back through the hole.

Her voice echoed back to him: "Pap?"

"Pass the holdall through. Take the cash out, leave everything else."

He dumped the bag by the side of the bed, and put the two keys of coke on Black's bloody chest like they were pinning him to the mattress.

He wiped his prints off the Desert Eagle and dropped it on the floor beside the bed. Let forensics have some fun piecing it together, he thought. The diamonds, the drugs, the guns. It looked like an execution to him, and when they put it all together—the grille on the floor, showing how the hit man got in and out, the phone call luring him away from the motel room—all of it would tell a story.

Tonya helped pull him through the air vent. He wriggled and struggled, trying to squeeze himself through the narrow opening despite the sheer agony it sent shooting through his shoulder. He clenched his teeth against the pain. Pain was temporary.

There was no way of knowing how long it would be before Black's body was discovered. A couple of minutes? A couple of hours? A couple of days? If the undercover cops had heard the shots, it'd be minutes rather than hours. If they hadn't, maybe he and Tonya would get to walk off into the sunset like cowboys at the end of the movie.

He couldn't control that.

What he could control was this: he took her in his arms, reached up to touch her cheek, and asked, "Do you love me?"

"Always have, you fool," she said, and kissed him.

He felt alive for the first time since Black had shot him.

"There's a sunset out there," he said, breaking the kiss. "Let's go watch it."

She didn't argue.

THE END

ABOUT THE AUTHORS

Albert Johnson

ALBERT "PRODIGY" JOHNSON, as one half of the multiplatinum rap group Mobb Deep, has sold millions of albums, performed throughout the world, and recorded with the elite of hip-hop, R&B, and rock with his signature style of hard-core, reality-based music. Born with the hereditary disease sickle-cell anemia, Prodigy has battled pain his entire life and is now promoting the importance of a healthy diet, spiritual enrichment, and a positive, productive lifestyle. He lives in Queens, New York.

Skary Ink

STEVEN SAVILE, a multiple finalist for the British Fantasy Award, has written for *Doctor Who, Torchwood, Primeval, Stargate, Warhammer, Sláine, Fireborn, Pathfinder,* and other popular game and comic series. He wrote the story for the international best-selling computer game *Battlefield 3,* which sold over five million copies in its first week of release, and served as head writer for the popular online children's game *Spineworld.*